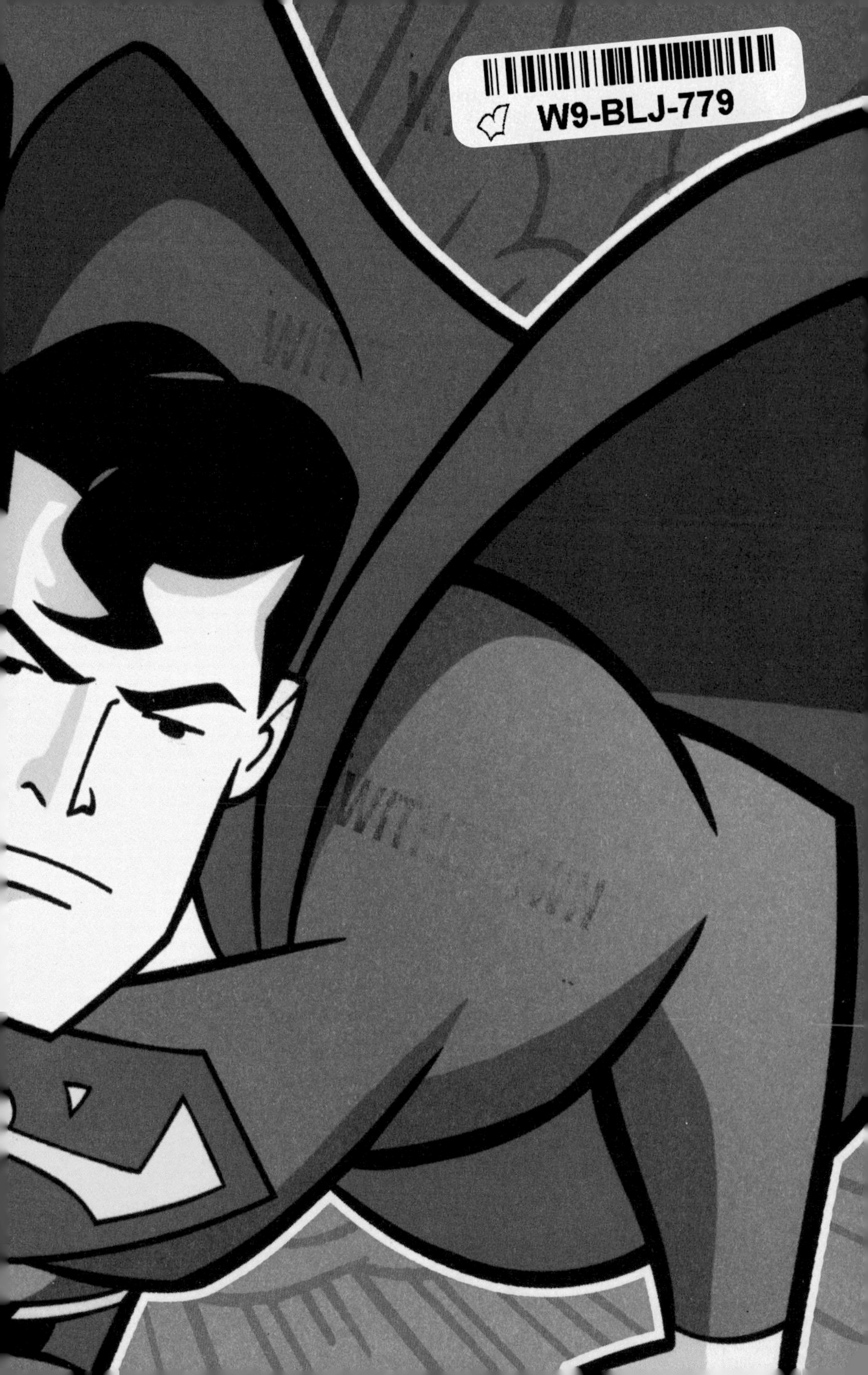

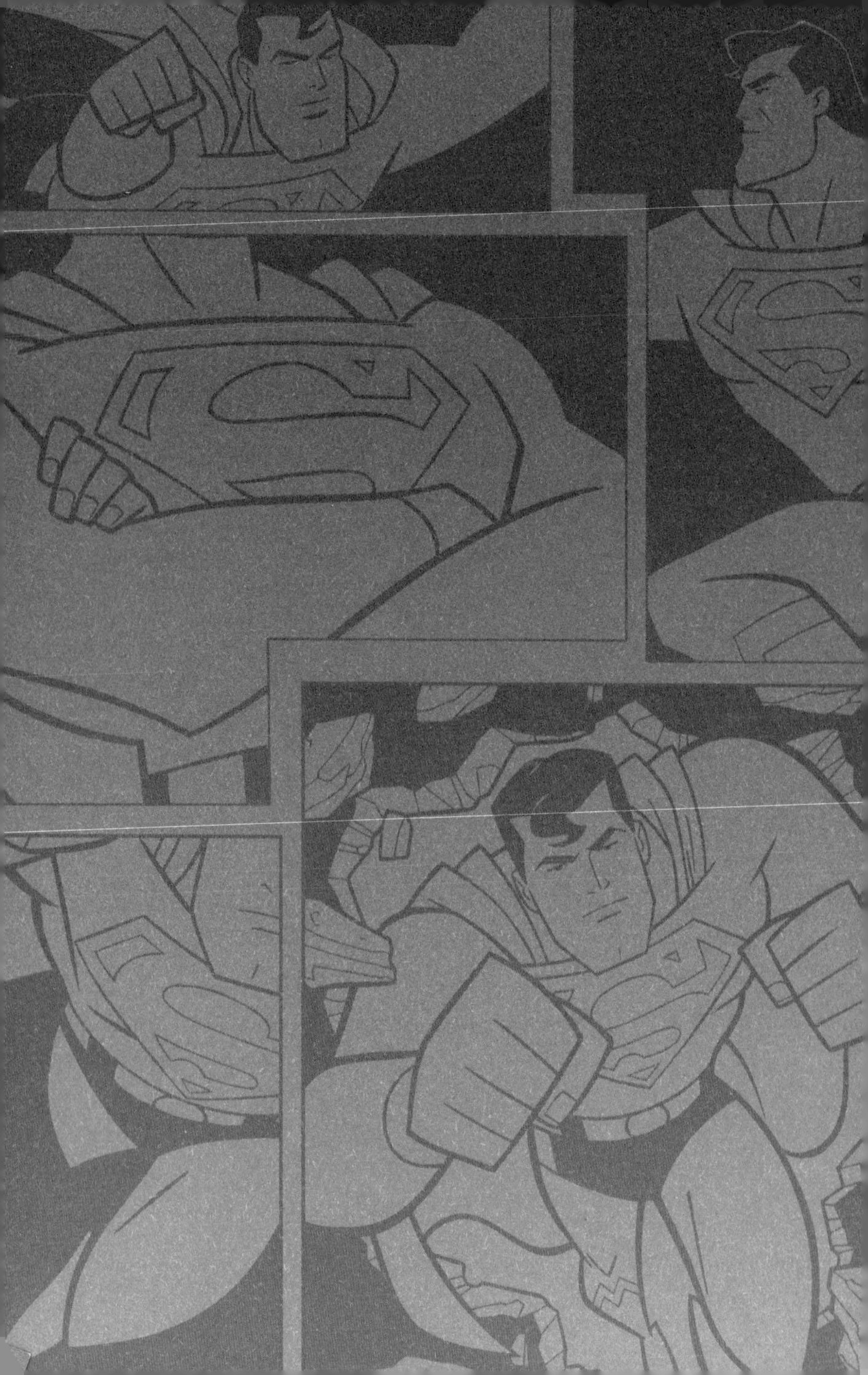

SUPER DC HEROES

SUPERMAN

METEOR of DOOM

WRITTEN BY
PAUL KUPPERBERG

ILLUSTRATED BY
SHAWN MCMANUS AND
LEE LOUGHRIDGE

SUPERMAN CREATED BY
JERRY SIEGEL AND
JOE SHUSTER

STONE ARCH BOOKS
MINNEAPOLIS   SAN DIEGO

Published by Stone Arch Books in 2010
151 Good Counsel Drive, P.O. Box 669
Mankato, Minnesota 56002
www.stonearchbooks.com

Library of Congress Cataloging-in-Publication Data

Kupperberg, Paul.
  Meteor of doom / by Paul Kupperberg ; illustrated by Shawn McManus.
    p. cm. -- (DC super heroes. Superman)
  ISBN 978-1-4342-1568-0 (lib. bdg.) -- ISBN 978-1-4342-1734-9 (pbk.)
  [1. Superheroes--Fiction.] I. McManus, Shawn, ill. II. Title.
  PZ7.K9523Me 2010
  [Fic]--dc22
                                      2009008740

Summary: Evil genius Lex Luthor is out to capture a deep space probe, which
has gathered a large kryptonite meteor! But Superman has been kept busy
protecting the city from a rash of crazy crimes. Can the super hero prevent
Luthor from getting his hands on the deadly rock?

Art Director: Bob Lentz
Designer: Brann Garvey

TABLE OF CONTENTS

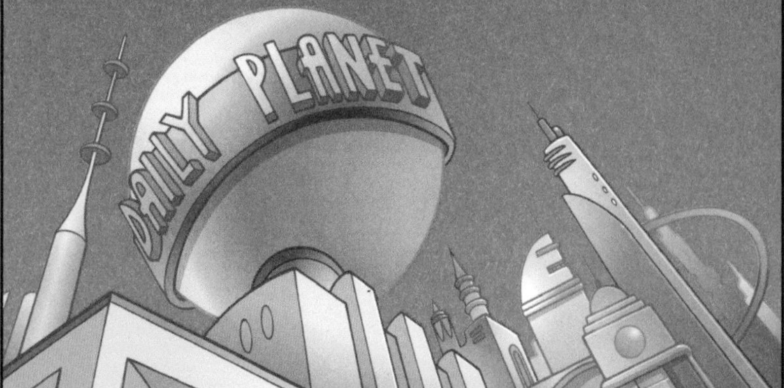
DAILY PLANET

CHAPTER 1

SURPRISE FROM THE SKY

LexCorp Tower stood in the center
of Metropolis. It was one of the tallest
buildings in the city and was named for
its owner, Lex Luthor. Luthor was one
of the richest businessmen in the world.
Thousands of people in Metropolis worked
for his companies.

Luthor enjoyed impressing people with
his money. When he wanted to announce
news about his company to reporters, he
did it from his private garden on the roof of
LexCorp Tower.

As the sun shined in the sky, Luthor stood in front of a microphone in the garden. Nearby was a large box-shaped device. It was covered with a dark blue sheet.

Clark Kent and Lois Lane were reporters for the Metropolis *Daily Planet* newspaper. They were just two of the many reporters there to hear Luthor's announcement. Clark had a pad of paper and pen in his hand to take notes.

"I wonder what Luthor is planning?" Lois said. "You know how he likes to make a big deal out of everything he does."

"He is a show-off," Clark admitted. "I just hope he doesn't take too long. I'm supposed to be at S.T.A.R. Laboratories. I'm covering the return of the Deep Space Probe for tomorrow's paper."

"The space mission?" Lois asked. "Aren't they bringing back meteors from orbit around Mars?"

"Yes," Clark said. "These will be the first meteors ever brought back from space! Before now, the only meteors scientists have been able to study were the ones that fell to Earth."

"Ladies and gentlemen," Luthor spoke into the microphone. "Thank you all for coming. As you know, LexCorp is always looking for ways to help the people of Metropolis. I am pleased to introduce our latest invention . . . the LexCorp Solar Generator!"

Luthor grasped the edge of the sheet that covered the mysterious box-shaped device. He paused for a moment and then tugged on the sheet.

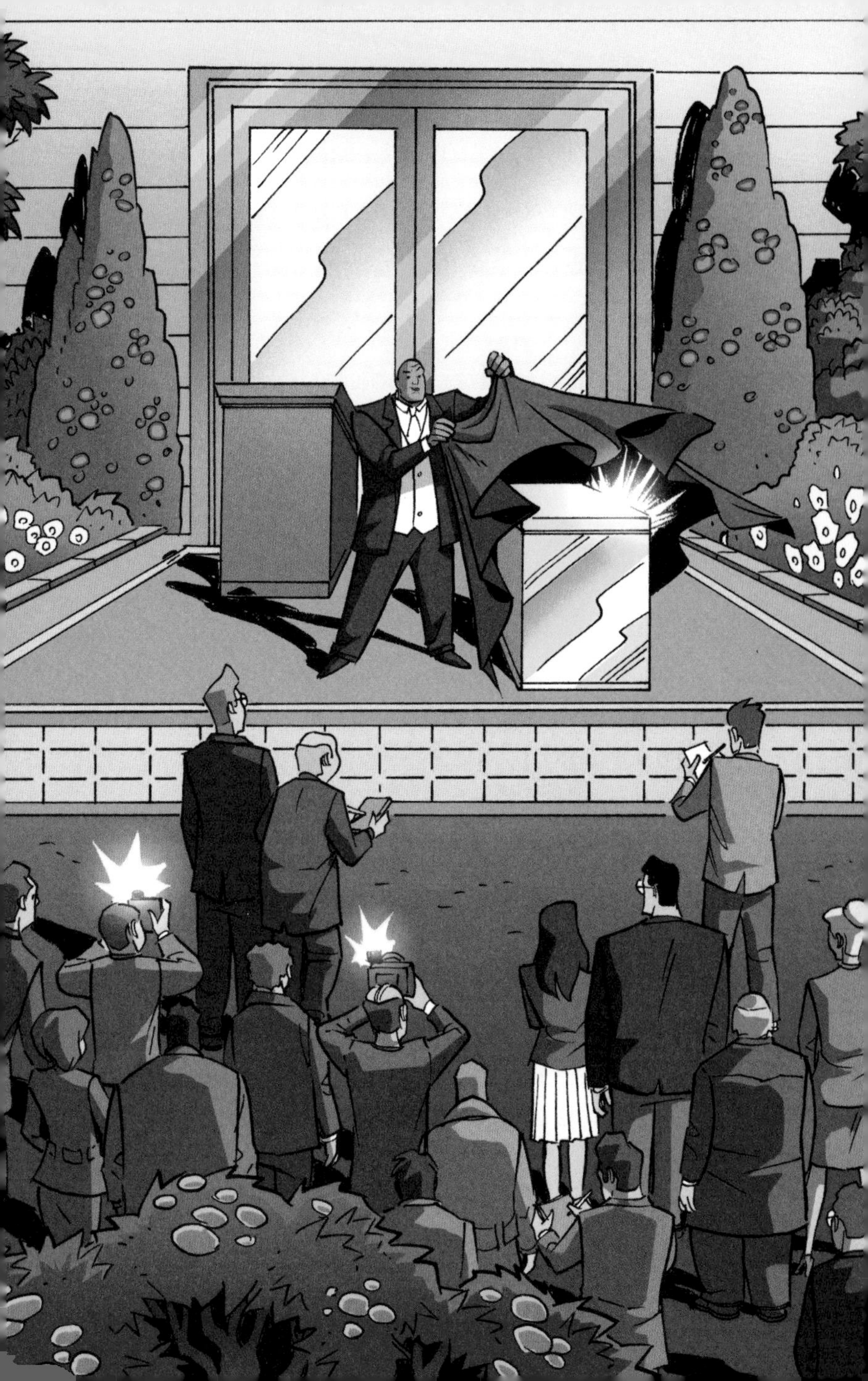

The sheet slid off the device, revealing a golden box with a shiny top. The top sparkled in the afternoon sunlight. Reporters leaned in for a closer look at the device. Photographers took pictures.

"The Solar Generator is a battery that stores energy from the sun," Luthor told the curious reporters. "That energy can be used to supply electricity for your entire house. And it costs only pennies a day!"

The excited reporters began to shout questions at Luthor. Clark Kent was not one of them. Instead, he stood still. His eyes were raised to the sky.

"What's wrong, Clark?" Lois asked.

"I thought I heard something," Clark said.

"I don't hear anything," said Lois.

Lois did not know that Clark Kent had secret abilities. He could hear and do things ordinary people could not.

Clark pointed upward. "There!" he said.

Lois thought he was pointing at a flock of birds flying toward the roof. As they came closer, she saw they were not birds. They were men — three of them — each wearing a rocket-powered flying suit!

Before Lois could say anything, Clark pushed her toward the elevators.

"Quick, Lois," he said. "You should get inside and call the police!"

"*You* call the police," Lois said. "I'm not going to miss out on this story!"

With his super-vision, Clark could see that the flying men were carrying energy blasters. There was no time to waste.

Clark ran to the elevator. As soon as the doors closed, the mild-mannered reporter pulled open his shirt. Beneath it was a blue uniform. It was marked with the famous red and yellow "S" symbol.

"This looks like a job," Clark said to himself, "for Superman!"

As Clark Kent changed into his Superman uniform, the flying men swooped down from the sky. They began firing their energy blasters at the people gathered on the rooftop.

BOOM! The first shot caused a bed of rare flowers to explode in a shower of dirt and flower petals.

BOOM! The next one shattered Luthor's Solar Generator into a thousand pieces of metal and glass.

KA-BOOM! KA-BOOM!

Two more blasts melted the microphone where Luthor had been standing just a moment before.

Luthor shook his fist at the flying men. "How dare you!" he yelled over the sound of the blasts. "Don't you know who I am?"

The reporters were also yelling, but they were shouting in fear and panic. While the other reporters were running away, Lois Lane ran toward the attack. She pulled a digital camera from her purse.

This is turning out to be a better story than I imagined! Lois thought.

Lois aimed the camera at one of the attackers. FLASH! She took a picture of the flying man. Then he turned and pointed at her.

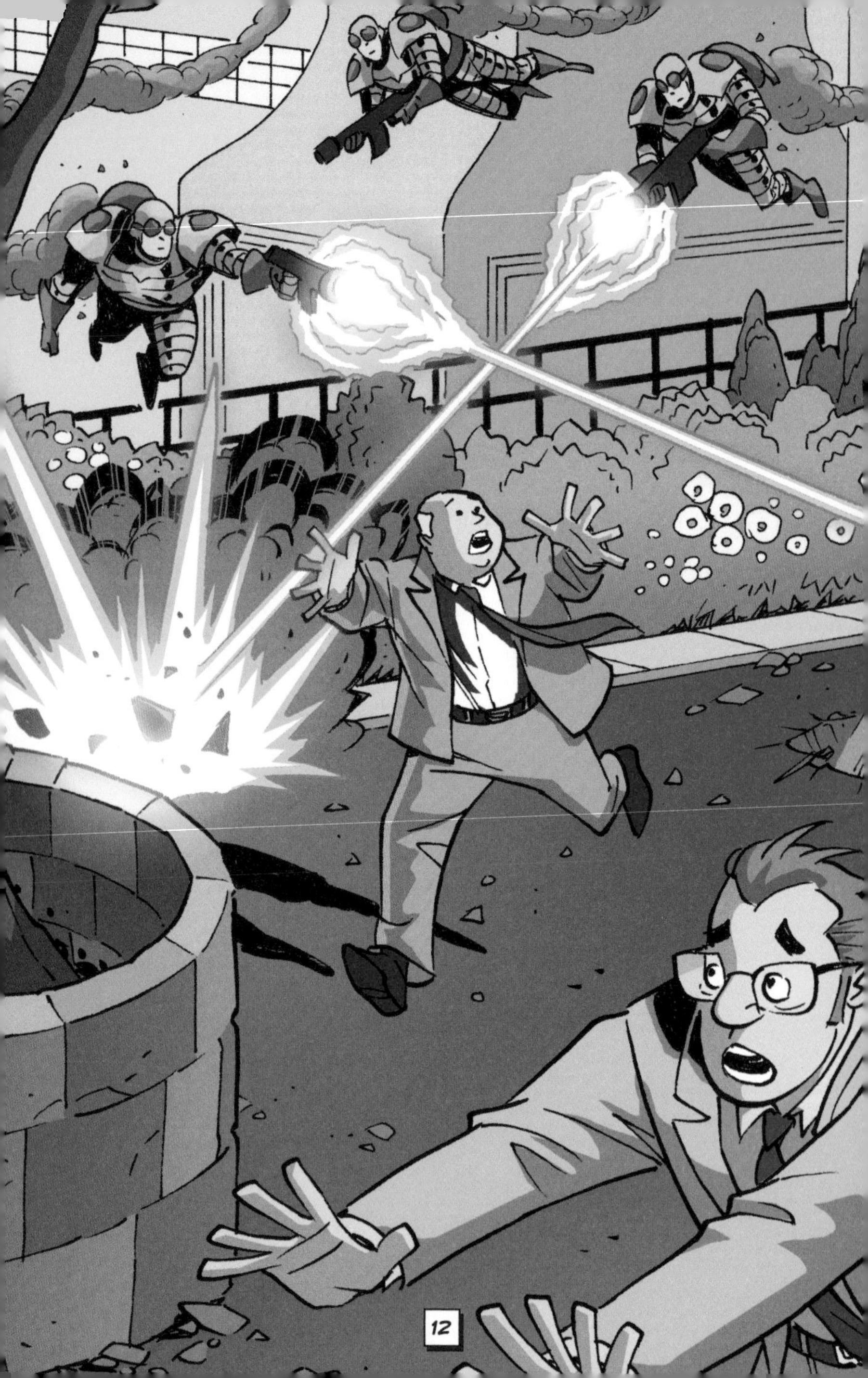

"There she is!" the flying man yelled to his companions. "Get her!"

"Uh-oh!" Lois said. She started to run. The flying men were speeding toward her from all sides. She was trapped!

CHAPTER 2

ATTACK ON METROPOLIS

The flying men were speeding toward Lois. There was nowhere to run. Then Superman swooped down from the sky and landed in front of her.

"Looks like you could use a hand, Lois," a familiar voice said.

Lois gasped in relief. "Superman!" she said.

The armored men were surprised by the sudden appearance of the super hero, but they did not slow down.

CRUNCH! The closest attacker smashed into Superman's chest. The man's armor broke open like a tin can. Superman did not budge from the impact.

Superman was born on the distant planet Krypton. He had been sent to Earth by his parents when Krypton exploded. The Earth's yellow sun made his alien body super-strong and super-fast. It also gave him other superpowers. He was invulnerable, which meant he could not be hurt like normal people. Only magic and kryptonite, a rare, glowing green rock from his home planet, could harm the Man of Steel.

Superman looked up at the second flying man. He narrowed his eyes. In an instant, beams of heat-vision flashed from the hero's eyes. **BZZT!**

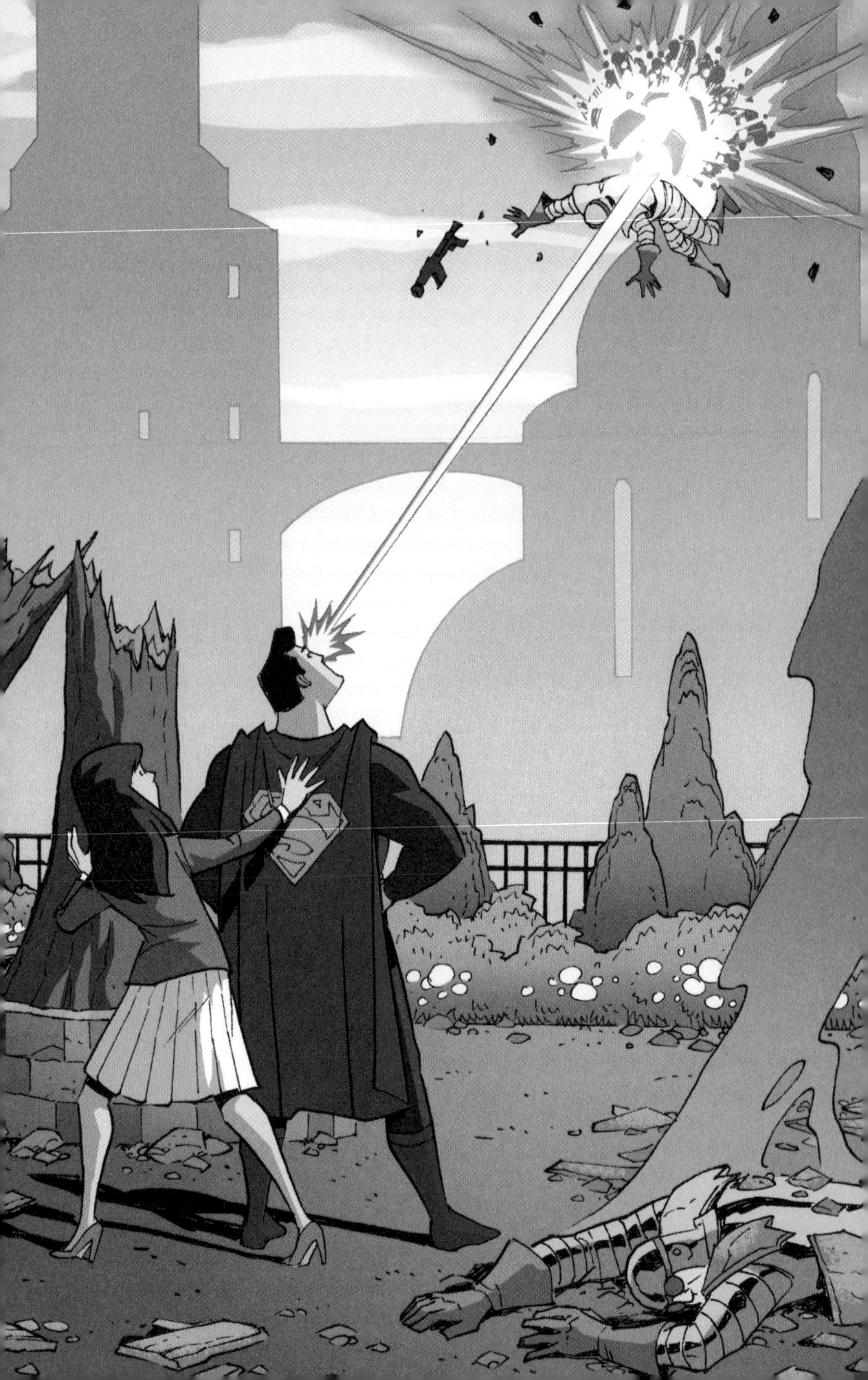

The beams struck the small rocket engine on the back of the flyer's armored suit. The engine caught fire. POP! POP! It sputtered and shut off. The armored man yelled in surprise. He fell to the rooftop like a rock.

"Superman, look out!" cried Lois.

The Man of Steel turned. He saw the last flying man aiming his energy blaster at him. Superman smiled and took a deep breath. He blew out a mighty blast from his super-powered lungs.

THWOOOOMMM!! The flying man was caught like a leaf in a hurricane. With a frightened scream, he was sent tumbling backward through the air. He landed with a crash, many miles away, right in front of the Metropolis police headquarters.

Superman turned to Lois and asked, "Are you all right, Miss Lane?"

"I am now, thanks to you," Lois said.

Lex Luthor came storming over to Superman and shouted, "There's nothing to thank him for, Ms. Lane! If he had gotten here faster, those villains wouldn't have destroyed my Solar Generator! And my beautiful garden is ruined!"

"You're just angry because Superman had to rescue you, Luthor," Lois said. "It's no secret how jealous you are that everyone in Metropolis thinks Superman's a bigger hero than you!"

"Lex Luthor is jealous of no man!" said the angry businessman.

"No, but you're sure jealous of a *super* man!" Lois said with a sly smile.

Superman was staring at the wreckage of the Solar Generator.

"Hmm," Superman said, before turning to Luthor. "I'm sorry I couldn't save your new machine, Luthor. Fortunately, no one was hurt in the attack."

"What about my garden?" Luthor bellowed.

"You can always grow new flowers," said the Man of Steel. "Now, if you'll excuse me, I have another appointment." He did not say that it was with S.T.A.R. Laboratories to report on the return of the Deep Space Probe as Clark Kent.

"Thanks again, Superman," Lois called as he flew away.

Superman waved and said, "Always happy to help, Lois."

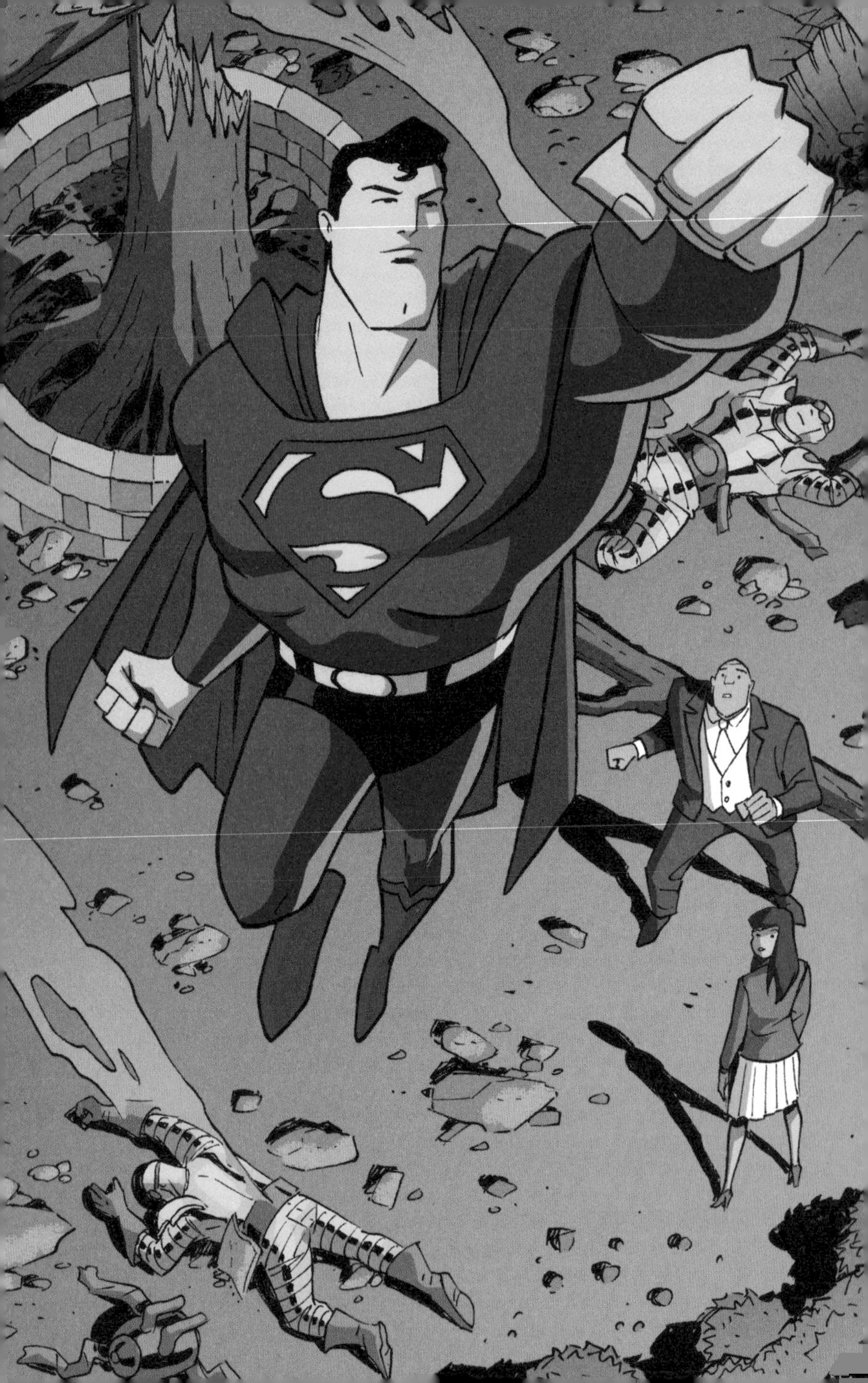

As he flew away, Superman knew that it wasn't jealousy that caused Luthor to hate him. It was because of the dark secret that Luthor kept hidden from the people of Metropolis. Behind his reputation as a businessman and inventor, Lex Luthor was the mastermind of a worldwide criminal empire!

So far, Luthor had been too smart to leave any evidence. Superman couldn't prove he was a criminal. Still, Luthor knew that if anyone could ever prove he was guilty, it would be the Man of Steel. Because of that, Luthor had vowed to destroy Superman.

Superman's thoughts were cut short by a sudden sound.

BEEP! BEEP! BEEP!

It was a special sound that only Superman's ears could hear. It was made by a signaling device that he had given to a close friend. Hearing it now meant only one thing.

Jimmy Olsen was in trouble!

CHAPTER 3

METAL MONSTER

WHAM! A giant metal foot bigger than a car smashed into the sidewalk right next to Jimmy Olsen. With a loud yelp of surprise, Jimmy jumped out of its way. The giant foot had missed him by inches!

The young man flattened himself against the side of a building. He looked up, and up, and up. His eyes traveled from the car-sized foot to a metal leg that was at least 30 feet tall. Then he saw a robot with gleaming eyes and arms as long as fire hoses.

"Wow!" Jimmy whispered in shocked surprise.

Only moments earlier, the young *Daily Planet* photographer had been strolling down the street. He was on his way to meet Clark Kent at the S.T.A.R. Laboratories Building. S.T.A.R. stood for Scientific and Technological Advanced Research. The smartest scientists from all over the world worked for S.T.A.R. They created scientific and medical marvels for the benefit of people everywhere.

Jimmy had been excited about this assignment. He was going to be allowed to take the very first pictures of the meteors being brought back from Mars on the Deep Space Probe!

But for now, the meteors would have to wait.

As soon as the giant robot had appeared in the street, Jimmy touched a signal button on his special wristwatch. Superman had given it to him. The button activated a supersonic danger signal that only Superman could hear.

CLICK! CLICK! Jimmy started snapping pictures of the robot. For a moment, the metal monster didn't notice. Seventy feet up in the air, its massive head turned back and forth. It seemed to be searching for something. Jimmy kept shooting pictures. CLICK! CLICK!

Suddenly, through the camera's viewfinder, Jimmy saw the robot's giant green eyes staring down at him. By the time he had lowered the camera from his face, the robot's metal hand was already reaching for him!

Jimmy gulped in fear and turned to run. He knew he could not possibly run fast enough to escape that giant hand. He had only one hope.

"Superman!" Jimmy exclaimed.

The Man of Steel arrived in the nick of time. He snatched Jimmy Olsen away from the robotic fingers.

"Relax, Jimmy," Superman said. He flew the young reporter up, up, and away from the robot. "You're safe now."

"Thanks, Superman," Jimmy stammered with relief. "I don't know why, but that big bucket of bolts seemed to be looking for me!"

"Hmm," Superman said thoughtfully. "I wonder why?"

"Beats me," said Jimmy with a shrug.

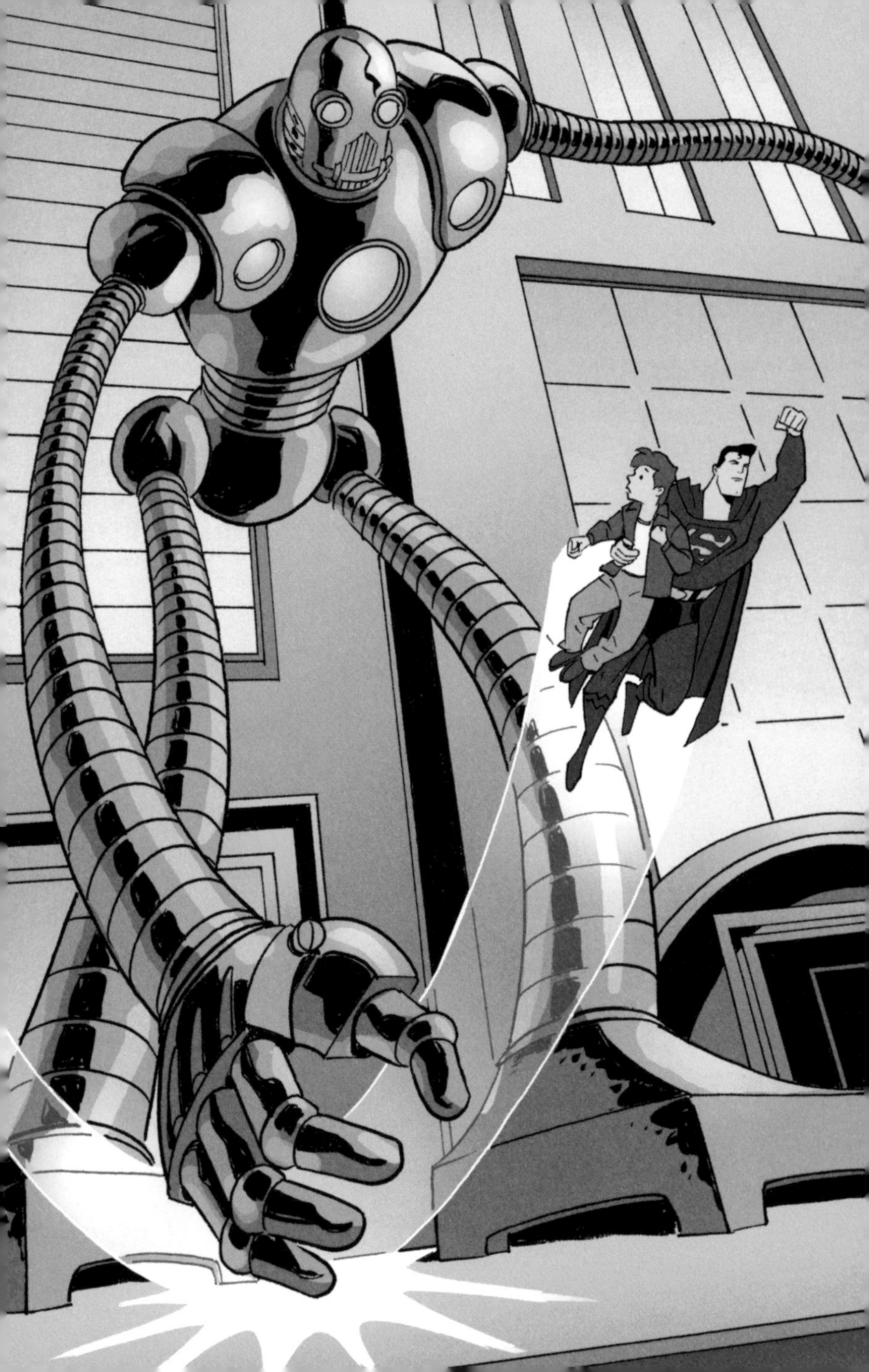

"I was just on my way to S.T.A.R. Labs," Jimmy continued. "I was going to take pictures of the Deep Space Probe for Clark Kent's story."

Superman set Jimmy back down on the sidewalk.

"First Lois Lane was attacked, and now you," Superman said.

"Is Miss Lane all right?" Jimmy asked.

"She's fine, Jimmy," Superman said. He stroked his chin. "Something strange is going on. I'll have to figure it out. But first, I have to stop that robot before somebody gets hurt!"

Before Jimmy could ask another question, Superman took off in a streak of red and blue.

The photographer raised his camera. He followed the Man of Steel through the viewfinder. He watched and took pictures as the super hero flew at the giant robot like a speeding missile.

Without pause, Superman tore through the side of the robot's metal head. Then he exploded out the opposite side.

Only then did Superman stop to see the result of his attack. The giant metal monster came to a dead stop. Smoke and sparks spilled from the holes in its head. The menacing green glow of its eyes blinked off. Then, like a mighty tree that had been chopped down, it started to fall. Superman was there to catch it. Gently, he laid it down on the street so it wouldn't do more damage.

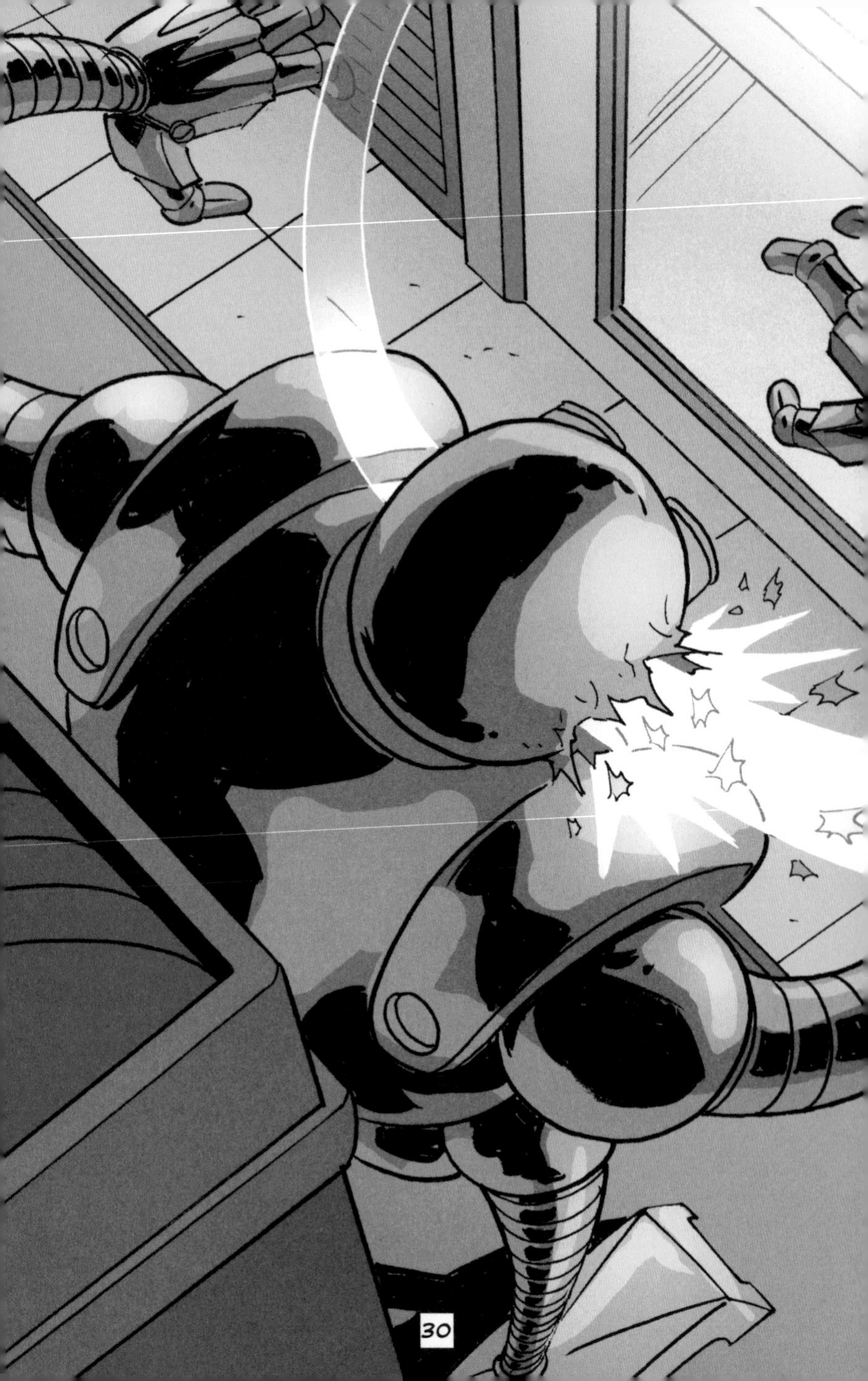

Jimmy was still taking pictures when he saw Superman's head suddenly snap up, listening. He knew the Man of Steel had heard something. In the next moment, Superman was gone.

THWOOOOMMMMMM!!

He had flown away at super-speed!

"Wow!" Jimmy whispered.

CHAPTER 4

FLYING SAUCERS

"Great Caesar's ghost!" Perry White, editor of the *Daily Planet*, yelled from the doorway of his office.

Everyone in the newsroom of the great metropolitan newspaper froze. When their boss yelled like that, they knew someone was in big trouble.

"I just heard from S.T.A.R. Labs," Perry shouted to no one in particular. "The Deep Space Probe is about to land, and Clark Kent's not there to cover the story! Where is he?!"

Before anyone could answer, a loud noise filled the air. **CRASH!** The windows all around the large room exploded in a shower of broken glass. Shards fell on desks and busy reporters. People shouted in surprise. Many dived under their desks for protection.

Through the broken windows came a swarm of small flying saucers. They were no bigger than dinner plates. They made angry buzzing noises as they flew. **BZZZZZZZZZZZZ**

One of the spinning saucers shot forward. It sliced through the computer monitor on a reporter's desk. **ZING!**

His face red with rage, Perry White stormed into the middle of the newsroom. "What do you think you're doing?" he shouted at the saucers. "Get out of here!"

The buzzing saucers reacted like living creatures to the sound of Perry's voice. They paused and then flew straight at him.

Perry stopped and stared. The flying saucers came toward him like a swarm of angry bees. *BZZT!*

"What the —" he started to shout, too surprised to move.

Just before the razor-sharp saucers reached him, a hand reached out from under a desk. It grabbed Perry's arm and yanked him to the floor. The swarming saucers buzzed past his head.

The hand that had dragged Perry to safety belonged to Ron Troupe. He was one of the newspaper's newest reporters.

"Looked like you needed a hand, boss," Ron said with a smile.

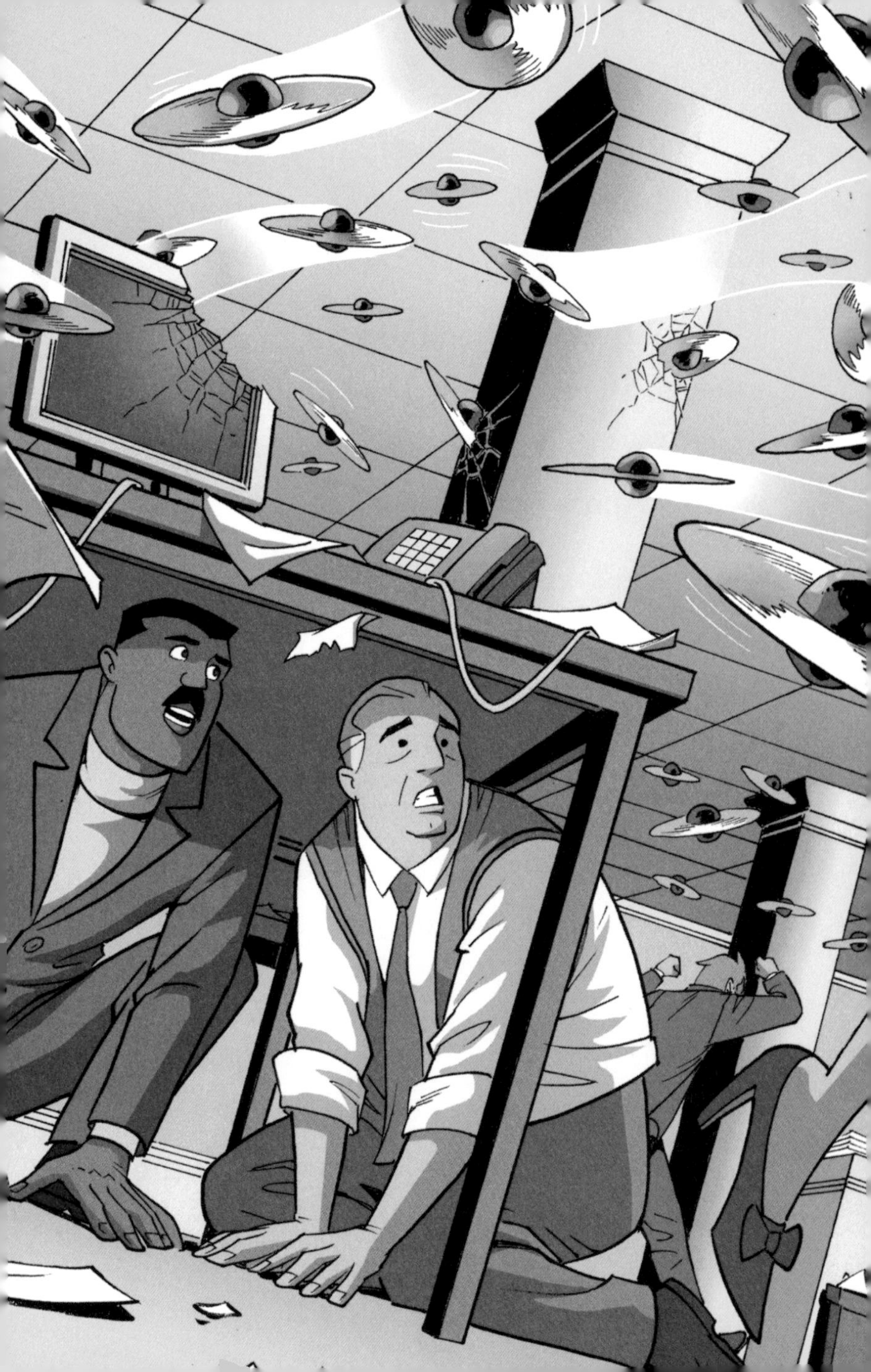

"Thanks, Troupe," Perry said. "Remind me about this the next time you ask for a raise."

Perry lifted his head to peek at the saucers. They continued to swirl around the room. "What the heck are those things?" he asked. "And what do they want?"

Once again, the saucers seemed to hear the sound of Perry's voice. They made a sudden, sharp turn and came whizzing back toward him. Perry's eyes went wide with fear. He threw himself flat on the floor. But this time, the saucers dived down after him. He realized that they were tracking him!

Perry threw his arms over his head and closed his eyes. There was no escape this time. All he could do was wait for the razor-sharp flying saucers to find him.

Suddenly, the newsroom was filled with the harsh, loud screech of tearing and bending metal. Perry opened his eyes.

He looked up in time to see Superman, standing between him and the saucers. Several of them were already bent and smashed. They rested in a heap on the floor at Superman's feet.

WHAM! Another one was crashing harmlessly against the Man of Steel's invulnerable chest.

SMASH! Superman punched another one from the air. **ZZRRRRTT!** The saucer clattered to the floor in a shower of sparks.

Superman shot his heat-vision at two saucers that were attacking Perry White. They instantly turned into melted hunks of metal.

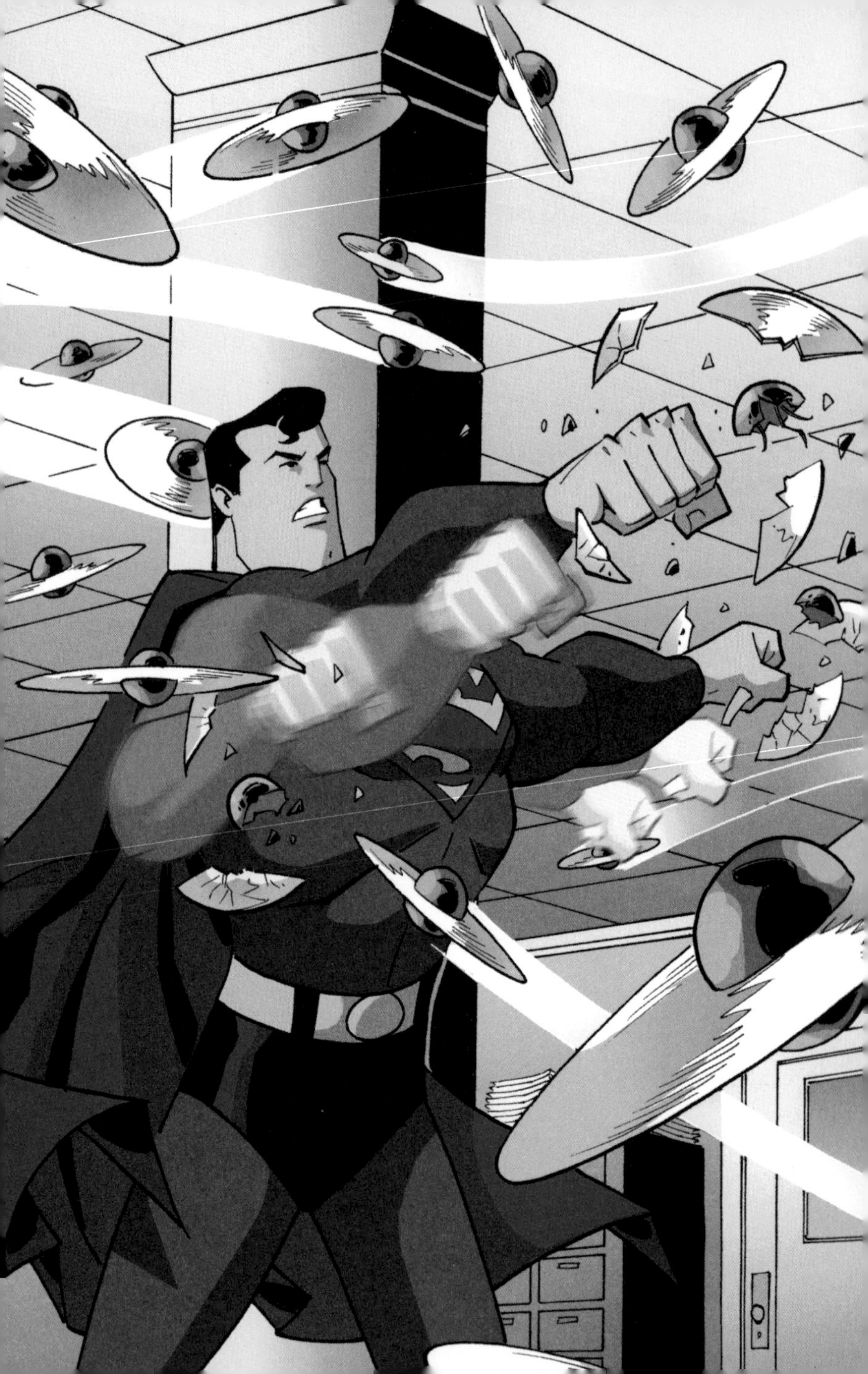

In a blur of super-speed punches, Superman smashed the remaining flying machines.

"Nice work, Superman," said Perry in relief. He rose to his feet, wiping his forehead with a handkerchief.

"Thank you," Superman said. "I wish I knew why my friends are being attacked. First Lois, then Jimmy, and now you."

"What about Clark Kent?" Perry asked with concern. "He's your friend too. And he never showed up at S.T.A.R. Laboratories. He could be in trouble!"

"Don't worry about Clark," Superman said with a smile. "I happen to know he's safe. And now, thanks to you, I think I know what's been going on!"

"That sounds like front-page news!" Perry said.

"It is," Superman said. "I'll make sure Clark Kent gets the whole story."

CHAPTER 5

FROM OUTER SPACE

The Deep Space Probe was blazing into the atmosphere high above Metropolis. It was traveling at many thousands of miles per hour. The thick layer of air surrounding Earth began to slow its speed.

Soon, the probe fell to a height of ten miles above the surface. A large parachute opened to slow it down even more. If all went according to plan, it would then float gently down to a soft, safe splash in Metropolis Harbor. Boats from S.T.A.R. Laboratories were waiting to pick it up.

At that same moment, S.T.A.R. Labs received a radio signal from the returning probe. Suddenly, the robot that Superman had defeated earlier came back to life!

Its large green eyes started to glow. The robot rose to its feet. It surprised the police and emergency crews who were trying to figure how to remove it from the street. Huge rocket engines in its feet roared to life. Like a missile, the robot blasted straight into the air.

Higher and higher it soared. Within seconds, it reached the Deep Space Probe, which was falling slowly to Earth beneath its large parachute. Like an outfielder catching a fly ball, the robot caught the probe in its giant hands. With its new prize, the robot began to return to Earth!

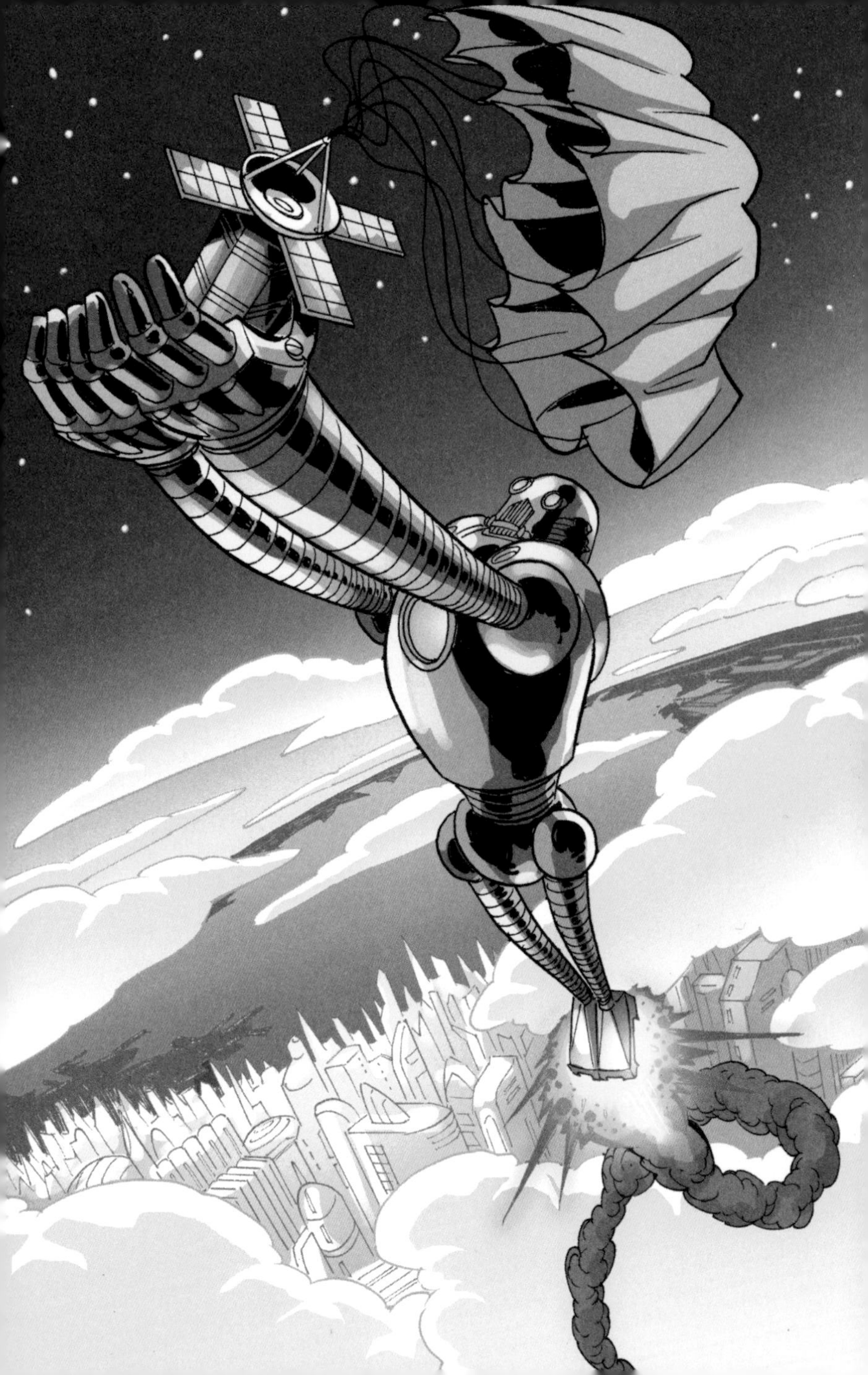

A tall figure stood in the shadows of a cavern beneath Metropolis. He waited patiently at the bottom of a large shaft that connected the cavern to the surface. He was waiting for something.

Sure enough, he heard the sound he was expecting. It was the clank of metal in the shaft.

"Come to me, my giant robot," the man whispered. He began to smile.

But the man's smile turned to surprise when the robot's head came tumbling out of the shaft! Wires and connecting rods dangled from beneath it. It had been torn from the robot's body.

The man jumped from the path of the tumbling head as it rolled across the cavern floor. It crashed against a rocky wall.

"What the devil?" the man growled.

"Not the devil," a voice echoed through the darkness of the shaft.

Superman came flying into the cavern. He landed in front of the man.

"Superman! What's the meaning of this?" the man asked. He was kneeling on the ground, brushing dirt from his dark suit. He stood up and stepped into the light.

It was Lex Luthor.

"I think you know, Luthor," Superman said. "After all, it was you who planned all those attacks on my friends to keep me busy. Meanwhile, your robot stole the Deep Space Probe."

Luthor smiled an evil smile. "I have no idea what you're talking about," he said.

"Having your men attack LexCorp first was clever," Superman said. "That way, I wouldn't suspect you. Not even after I checked the wreckage of your so-called Solar Generator with my X-ray vision. I wondered why you were showing reporters a fake machine made of useless parts."

"That proves nothing," said Luthor.

"Only you could have built those armored suits, and the flying saucers that attacked Perry White," said Superman. "And a robot with two computer-brains! You knew I would smash the one in its head to stop it. The second brain was in its chest. That one was programmed to steal the Space Probe!"

"What would I want with a ship full of space rocks?" asked Luthor with a sneer.

"Somehow you discovered that one of the meteors the probe was bringing back to Earth was made of kryptonite," said Superman. "That's the one thing in the universe that can kill me!"

"Hmm," said Luthor. "I suppose the spaceship was lined with lead. That protected you from the kryptonite when you took the probe from the robot. Do you have any proof I did any of these things?"

"No. As usual, you were very clever," said Superman. "One day you'll make a mistake. When you do, I'll be waiting."

Luthor grinned. "In that case, I'll be going now," he said.

Superman smiled back. "One last thing, Luthor," he said. "I'm afraid I smashed the elevator on my way down."

"What?" said Luthor.

"Since you're such a genius, I'm sure you'll figure out how to fix it," said Superman. "Or you can just use the ladder. It's only a mile to the top!"

Superman waved and flew off. He disappeared into the dark shaft that led back to Metropolis.

Luthor growled. He could still hear the Man of Steel's laughter as he started the long climb to the top.

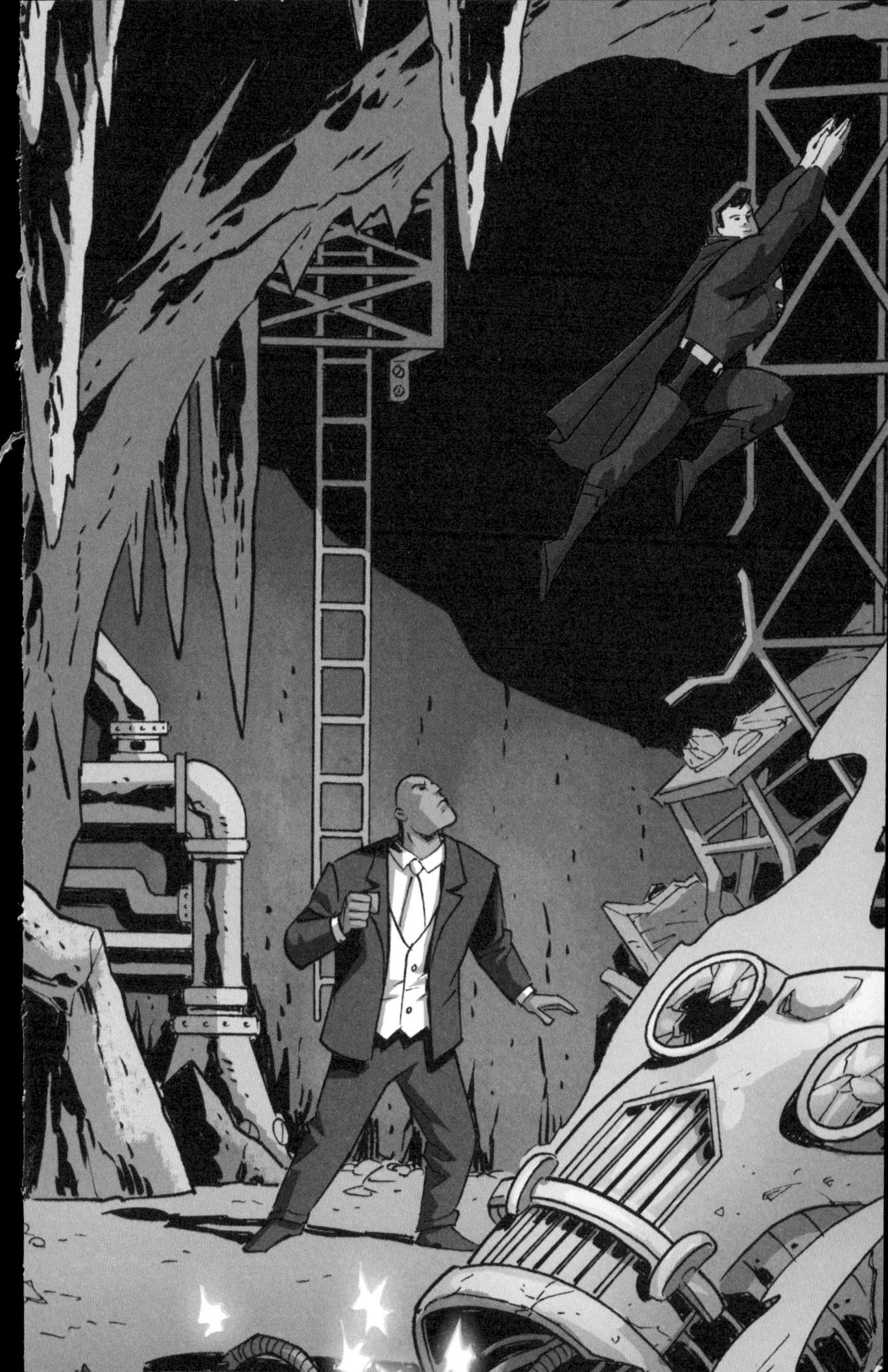

DAILY PLANET

WHO IS LEX LUTHOR?

Lex Luthor is one of the richest and most powerful people in all of Metropolis. He's known as a successful businessman to most, but Superman knows Luthor's dirty little secret — most of his wealth is ill-gotten, and behind the scenes he is a criminal mastermind. Superman has stopped many of Luthor's sinister schemes, but Lex is careful to avoid getting caught red-handed. Lex wants to control Superman to strengthen his grip on Metropolis, but the Man of Steel is immune to Luthor's influence.

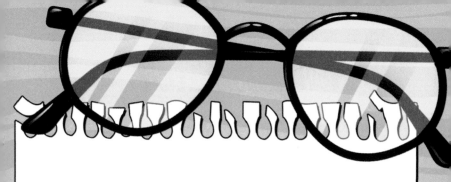

- While Lex Luthor lacks superpowers of his own, he is a scientific genius and a criminal mastermind. He has often enlisted the help of super-villains in his quest to topple the towering Man of Steel.

- Before Superman came to Metropolis, Lex Luthor tried to win Lois Lane's heart by any means necessary. But Lois did not return the businessman's love, having found hints of his corruption over the years in her role as a reporter.

- Luthor has gone to extreme lengths to defeat Superman. He transformed John Corben into a cybernetic monster! Lex failed to use the metal man, named Metallo, to bend the Man of Steel to his will. And when the villainess Livewire was short-circuited by Superman, it was Lex who shocked her back to life.

- In an attempt to become even more powerful, Lex schemed his way into the office of President of the United States! It ended badly for him, however, when citizens discovered that he intentionally put the world at risk to increase his approval ratings.

BIOGRAPHIES

Paul Kupperberg has written many books for kids, like *Powerpuff Girls: Buttercup's Terrible Temper Tantrums* and *Hey, Sophie!* He has also written more than 600 comic book stories involving Superman, the Justice League, Spider-Man, Hulk, Scooby Doo, *Star Trek*, and many others. Paul's own character creations include Arion: Lord of Atlantis, Checkmate, and Takion. He has also been an editor for DC Comics, *Weekly World News*, and World Wrestling Entertainment. Paul lives in Connecticut with his wife Robin, son Max, and dog, Spike.

Shawn McManus has been drawing pictures ever since he was able to hold a pencil. He has illustrated the comic book characters Sandman, Batman, Dr. Fate, Spider-Man, and many others. Shawn has also done work for film, animation, and online entertainment. He lives in New England, and he loves the spring season there.

Lee Loughridge has been working in comics for more than 14 years. He currently lives in sunny California in a tent on the beach.

GLOSSARY

companion (kuhm-PAN-yuhn)—a companion is someone you spend a lot of time with

device (di-VISSE)—a piece of equipment that does a particular job

evidence (EV-uh-duhnss)—information or items that help prove something

massive (MASS-iv)—huge or heavy

mastermind (MASS-tur-minde)—a highly intelligent person who thinks up complicated plans

menacing (MEN-iss-ing)—threatening or dangerous

meteor (MEE-tee-ur)—a piece of rock or metal from space that falls into the Earth's atmosphere

shattered (SHAT-urd)—broke something into tiny pieces

villains (VIL-uhnz)—wicked or evil people

vowed (VOUD)—made a serious or important promise

DISCUSSION QUESTIONS

1. More than anything, Lex Luthor wants to destroy the Man of Steel. Why do you think Lex wants to get rid of Superman so badly?

2. Clark Kent's secret identity is Superman. If you were a super hero, would you keep your identity a secret? Why or why not?

3. Superman knew Lex was guilty, but he didn't arrest him because he had no proof. Would you have let Lex go free? Why or why not?

WRITING PROMPTS

1. Superman pretends to be a normal human being. Do you ever pretend to be something or someone you're not? Do you know anyone who does? Write about it.

2. Imagine you're a famous reporter like Lois Lane or Clark Kent. Write a newspaper article about the events that occurred in this story. Make sure to use a catchy headline.